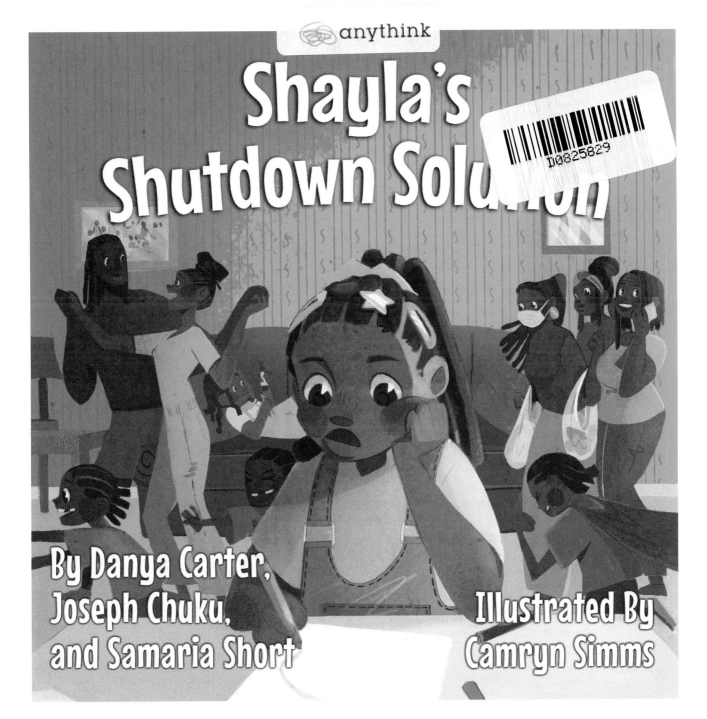

Shayla's Shutdown Solution

By Danya Carter, Joseph Chuku, and Samaria Short

Illustrated By Camryn Simms

Reach Incorporated | Washington, DC

Shout Mouse Press

Reach Education, Inc. / Shout Mouse Press
Published by
Shout Mouse Press, Inc.

Shout Mouse Press is a nonprofit writing and publishing program dedicated to amplifying underheard voices. This book was produced through Shout Mouse workshops and in collaboration with Shout Mouse artists and editors.

Shout Mouse invites young people from marginalized backgrounds to tell their own stories in their own voices and, as published authors, to act as leaders and agents of change. In partnership with other mission-aligned nonprofits, we are building a catalog of inclusive books that ensure that all children can see themselves represented on the page. Our 300+ authors have produced original children's books, comics, novels, memoirs, and poetry collections.

Learn more and see our full catalog at www.shoutmousepress.org.

Copyright © 2020 Reach Education, Inc.
ISBN-13: 978-1-950807-13-0 (Shout Mouse Press, Inc.)

All rights reserved. No part of this book may be reproduced or transmitted in any form or by any means, electronic or mechanical, including photocopying, recording, or by an information storage and retrieval system, without written permission from the publisher, excepting brief quotes used in reviews.

To all the kids who need their space,
during the pandemic
and otherwise.

Hey there! I'm Shayla!

I'm eight years old. I like to read and draw pictures of flowers, animals, and houses in my neighborhood. One day I'm going to be a famous artist!

But right now it's not always easy for me...

...and let me tell you why.

I have a big family. And by big, I mean BIG!
I live with Mommy and Daddy...

...and my three brothers, three sisters, three aunties,
and my three little cousins: Aiden, Jayden, and Hayden.

I love them SO much, but the trouble is...

They are ALWAYS in the way. Especially now.

When I want to read in my room, my cousins are there playing dress-up, or playing with noisy toy cars, or running around playing tag.

When I want to draw at the kitchen table, half the grown folks in the house are there video-chatting for work.

And when I just want to be by myself, somebody's always calling my name to...

look for the remote...

do the dishes...

watch
my cousins...

...and more.

And, on top of that, I have schoolwork to do.
Right now, I have a project I need to finish.
I'm supposed to be drawing a logo for art class.
It's supposed to represent what matters most to me.

But it's been hard with everyone around all the time.

I want to ask for space and time to do my own thing,
but everyone is so stressed and busy.
I feel like I cannot bother them.

My cousins already ruined my first logo by drawing all over it.
They said they were "trying to help."
But now I have to start over for the second time!
So, I sit down with all my materials and I begin to draw...
Aiden, Jayden, and Hayden sit down near me to drink their juice.
Soon, they get rowdy and Jayden knocks his cup over right onto my poster!

I lose my temper and throw all my markers at the wall.
"I hate it here!" I shout.

My Aunties hear me shout.

"Shayla, sit down and let's talk," they say.

"It's okay to be angry," says Auntie Cici.

"But you have to learn how to respond when things don't go your way," says Auntie Kiki.

"Let's talk about what's bothering you," says Auntie Titi.

I think about it for a minute...

"I just need space to do my project. Everyone is at home all the time right now. I'm tired of it!"

My Aunties nod. "We understand," Auntie Cici says. "We're ALL tired of this!"

"You just need to learn how to ignore people," Auntie Titi says.

So, I try that.

I sit on the couch to try drawing again.

My brothers are also there. They are playing video games and shouting at the TV.

And as much as I try to ignore them...

...it doesn't work.

I go back to my Aunties and tell them I am having a hard time.

Auntie Kiki says, "Why don't you try sitting in the hall closet away from everybody?"

So, I try that.

I go sit in the closet with a flashlight.

And it is great! Until...

...my sisters decide it's a perfect hideout for their dolls.
So, that doesn't work either.

I go back to my Aunties one more time. Auntie Cici suggests, "Why don't you try using headphones?"

So, I try that.
I think that nobody will bother me in the bathroom.
I put on headphones and listen to Beyonce and Tupac.
But then...

...my tablet dies.

I look everywhere for an outlet but they are all used up.
Even in the bathroom! So, that doesn't work either.

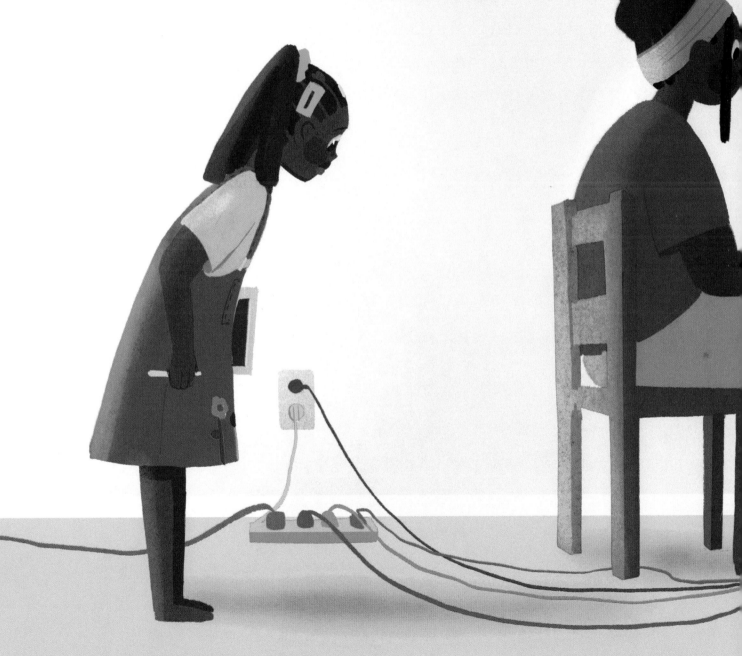

I get so frustrated that I start to cry.

The only place I can find to be alone is the stairwell of our apartment building.

But, even there, people come up and down...

...like Mommy and Daddy.

"What's wrong?" they ask.

I explain what's been going on. They listen and decide to call for a family meeting.

At the family meeting, Mommy says, "I know we're all struggling here. It's hard that we're all home. But Shayla can't get her schoolwork done with all the noise. How can we support her?"

My Auntie Kiki says, "We've suggested three different things to try and help, but none of them seem to work."

"We're sorry. We didn't know we were bothering you so much. We just wanted to play," says my little cousin Hayden.

"Yeah, we're sorry for being loud all the time," says one of my brothers.

"That's okay. I'm sorry too," I say.

My family keeps trying to come up with solutions, but nothing seems to make everyone happy.

Suddenly, I have an epiphany!

"What if I can have just ONE HOUR to myself every day when no one can bother me?"

The family all comes together in a circle to discuss.

"We can make that happen," says Auntie Cici.

After the family meeting, Auntie Kiki takes me aside to say, "I'm so proud of you for coming up with this solution on your own!"

When I hear that, I smile really big.

The next day, I wake up excited to work on my project.

All day long, while the adults work on their computers, I hang out with my sisters and we do each other's hair. That's the best way to pass a long time waiting.

Finally, at 4 p.m., my hour starts.

Everybody has to find some other place to be, because I need to use the kitchen table.

I get my markers and paper together and I get started!

I've been thinking about my design all day.

First I draw a diamond pattern with my three
favorite colors: blue and pink and burgundy.
Then, in big bubble letters, I write "Family."

When I'm done, I show my family and they love it!

My family is BIG, but that also makes them the BEST.
I can ask my family for help whenever I need it.
Even when what I really need is to have my own space!
Family Time is always great...

...but Me Time makes Family Time even better!

About the Authors

Danya Carter

I'm Danya Carter. I'm a 16-year-old 11th grader at Anacostia High School. When there's not a pandemic, I like to go to the mall with friends or go to parks with my family. I hope this book helps young readers learn about problem solving and good communication.

Joseph Chuku

I'm Joseph Chuku. I'm 17 years old and a junior at Calvin Coolidge High School. I like to work on cars and to watch medieval movies and shows on Netflix. I wanted to write this book because there wasn't anything like it! I want parents to know that it's okay to listen to kids. And I want kids to know that their feelings matter, and it's okay to speak up.

Samaria Short

I'm Samaria Short. I'm 15 years old and go to Eastern High School. I like to draw and paint anything, especially people and landscapes. This is my first book with Reach and Shout Mouse. I wanted to write this book because I like to express myself with art, and now I get to do it with words! I hope that when kids read our book they learn that it's okay to ask for help when you need it.

Sarai Johnson served as Story Coach for this book.

Hayes Davis served as Head Story Coach for this year's series.

About the Illustrator

Camryn Simms

Camryn is an illustrator pursuing a BFA in Communication Arts at Virginia Commonwealth University. Her love for comics and picture books growing up has led her to have a special place in her heart for visual storytelling. She is passionate about vivid artwork that engages the imagination. She enjoys working in a variety of different mediums, and ultimately, she hopes that readers can connect to her work and take away something meaningful.

Writers and artists at work

Acknowledgments

For the eighth summer in a row, teens from Reach Incorporated were issued a challenge: compose original children's books that will both educate and entertain young readers. Specifically, these teens were asked to create inclusive stories that reflect their lived experiences — experiences that this year include the current global pandemic and the struggle for racial justice. As always, these teens have demonstrated that they know their audience, they believe in their mission, and they take pride in the impact they can make on young lives.

Thirteen writers spent the month of July brainstorming ideas, generating potential plots, writing, revising, and providing critiques. Authoring quality books is challenging work at any time, but this year, these young people had to collaborate virtually, during a COVID-19 shutdown. These authors have our immense gratitude and respect: Jocktavious, Daveena, Geralyn, Shatyia, Japan, Damarco, Emilie, Riley, Anthony, Diarou, Danya, Joseph, and Samaria.

These books represent a collaboration between Reach Incorporated and Shout Mouse Press, and we are grateful for the leadership provided by members of both teams. From Reach, Anyssa Dhaouadi, Victoria Feathersone, and Charles Walker contributed meaningfully to discussions and morale, and the Reach summer program leadership of Jusna Perrin kept us organized and connected, even while we all worked apart. From the Shout Mouse Press team, we thank Head Story Coach Hayes Davis, who oversaw this year's workshops, and Story Coaches Barrett Smith, Sarai Johnson, Faith Campbell, and Alexa Patrick for bringing both fun and insight to the project. We can't thank enough illustrators Camryn Simms, Anthony White, Alex Perkins, and Rob Gibsun for bringing these stories to life with their beautiful artwork. Finally, Amber Colleran brought a keen eye and important mentorship to the project as the series Art Director and book designer. We are grateful for the time and talents of these writers and artists!

Finally, we thank those of you who have purchased books and cheered on our authors. It is your support that makes it possible for these teen authors to engage and inspire young readers. We hope you smile as much while you read as these teens did while they wrote.

Mark Hecker,
Reach Incorporated

Kathy Crutcher,
Shout Mouse Press

About Reach Incorporated

Reach

Reach Incorporated develops readers and leaders by preparing teens to serve as tutors and role models for younger students, resulting in improved literacy outcomes for both the teen tutors and their elementary school students.

Founded in 2009, Reach recruits high school students to be elementary school reading tutors. After completing a year in our program, teens gain access to additional leadership development opportunities, including The Summer Leadership Academy and The College Mentorship Program. All of this exists within our unique, college and career preparation framework, The Reach Fellowship. Through this comprehensive system of supports, teens are prepared to thrive in high school and beyond.

Through their work as reading tutors, our teens noticed that the books they read with their students did not always reflect their lived experiences. As always, we felt the best way we could address this issue was to put our teens in charge. Through our collaboration with Shout Mouse Press, these teens create engaging stories with diverse characters that invite young readers to explore the world through words. By purchasing our books, you support student-led, community-driven efforts to improve educational outcomes in the District of Columbia.

Learn more at www.reachincorporated.org.

Made in the USA
Monee, IL
19 December 2020

54721287R00024